I Am

I Am a Dancer

I Am

I Am a Dancer

ELEANOR SCHICK

MARSHALL CAVENDISH   NEW YORK

Library of Congress Cataloging-in-Publication Data
Schick, Eleanor, (date)
I am: I am a dancer / by Eleanor Schick.
p.   cm.
Summary: A young girl expresses her feelings about
herself and the world around her through dance.
ISBN 0-7614-5097-1
[1. Dance—Fiction.] I. Title.
PZ7.S3445 Iad 2001   [E]—dc21   00-047423

The text of this book is set in 27 point Bernhard Modern.
The illustrations are rendered in colored pencil.
Printed in Hong Kong
First edition
6   5   4   3   2   1

For Andrea,
Daniella, and
Sierra

*T*oday the sunlight
streams into my room
like a curtain of gold.

It feels warm
on my skin.

I am a cat
stretching in the sun.

I am the sun.

I am a dog
barking at danger
to protect my home.

Somewhere there is a meadow
with hundreds of flowers.

I am a flower
almost blooming.

A black stallion
is running free
across the land.

I am a black stallion.

I am clouds
floating over
rivers and canyons.

I am the ocean
crashing my waves

against the rocky shore.

I am a thousand white birds
flying everywhere
into the sky.

I am the moon,
still and silvery
in the night.

I am every child
in the world
dancing right now.

I am dreaming of
things that can be . . .

I am the dreamer
and I am the dream.

I am me.